Little Golden Books

Little Golden Books

Little Golden Books

Little Golden Books

Little Golden Books

A GOLDEN BOOK • NEW YORK

The Doc McStuffins television series was created by Chris Nee.

randomhouse.com/kids

ISBN 978-0-7364-3257-3

MANUFACTURED IN CHINA

10 9 8 7 6 5 4 3 2 1

a Little Golden Book® Collection

Disney Junior

Nine
FAVORITE
Tales

A GOLDEN BOOK • NEW YORK

CONTENTS

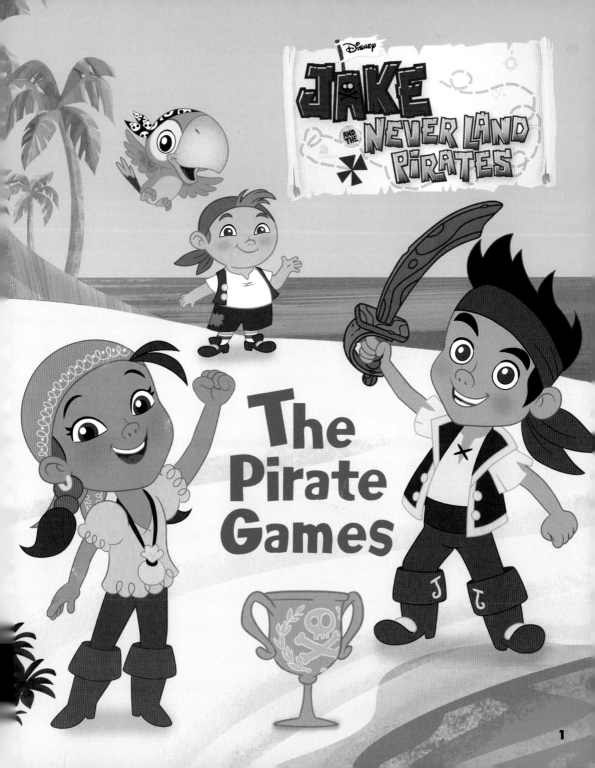

The Pirate Games

It's an exciting day on Pirate Island. Jake, Izzy, and Cubby are going to compete against Captain Hook's crew in the Never Land Pirate Games.

The team that wins gets a special treasure—a golden pirate trophy!

"Smee! I want that golden trophy thing!" Hook yells to his first mate.

The first event is the rope climb. "You have to climb to the top and ring the bell," explains Jake.

Izzy will climb for Jake's team. She loves climbing.

Hook orders Bones to do the climbing
for his team. But Bones is afraid of heights.

Izzy and Bones stand by their ropes. Jake starts the competition by calling out, "Ready? Yo, ho! Let's go!"

Izzy uses all her strength to pull herself up the rope. "I'm going to make it to the top," she tells herself as her teammates cheer her on.

Bones is barely off the ground. "It's scary, Cap'n!" he says to Hook.

Before long, Izzy reaches
the platform and rings the bell.
"Izzy wins!" cries Skully.

Captain Hook isn't happy. "Barnacles!" he hollers at Bones, who is all tangled up in his rope. "I'm not going to get the trophy like that!"

Now it's time for
the water cannon
target event. Cubby is
going first. He aims his
cannon, and . . .

SPLASH! Cubby knocks down the target.
"Bull's-eye!"cries Skully.

Next it's Smee's turn. He is trying to concentrate, but his teammates are making him nervous.

"Hit it here," Sharky calls out as he
and Bones jump around the target.
"You better not miss!" Hook yells,
and then glares at Smee.

Smee closes his eyes and squirts his water cannon. "Did I hit the target?" he asks.

"No, Smee!" hollers Hook as he gets knocked over by the stream of water. "I am not the target!"

For the last event, the teams head to an old pirate ship on the edge of the beach. "This is the pirate balance challenge," Cubby tells everyone.

"You have to walk across the ship's mast without falling."

Hook decides he will do this event himself.

But first it is Jake's turn. He holds his arms out to the sides, looks straight ahead, and carefully walks across the mast.

"Way to go, Jake!" cheers Cubby.
"Yay, hey! You did it!" yells Izzy.

"Bah! I can keep my balance, too," says Hook as he stands on the mast. The captain takes a few steps and starts to wobble.

Then the wobbling turns into falling!
"Help me, Smee!" cries Hook.

Once Captain Hook is fished out of the water, Jake and his crew begin to celebrate their win.

"Oh, dear, Cap'n," says Smee. "It looks like we lost."

"And I really wanted that golden trophy thing," Hook whines.

Jake, Izzy, and Cubby are proud of themselves. They worked well as a team and won the Never Land Pirate Games! Maybe they'll even let Hook borrow their trophy one day. . . .

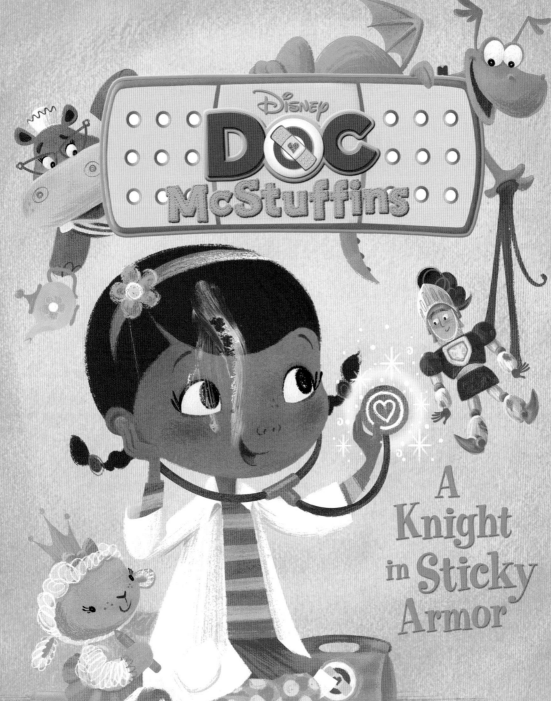

A
Knight
in Sticky
Armor

"Hi, everyone," Doc McStuffins says to her toys Lambie, Hallie, and Stuffy. Doc's stethoscope begins to glow—and her toys magically come to life. "Let's play princess," she declares.

Lambie loves playing princess. She pretends to be trapped in a castle. "Oh, save me, brave prince!" she cries.

Stuffy is playing the part of the brave prince. He runs toward the castle to rescue the princess but trips on a crayon and falls down. Luckily, Hallie is there to help Stuffy get up.

"Wouldn't it be perfect if we had a real knight in **shining** armor to save me?" Lambie asks from the top of the castle.

Doc thinks that is a good idea. She remembers that her little brother used to play with a toy knight all the time. "I'll see if we can borrow Donny's knight," Doc says.

"I remember that knight," Lambie tells Stuffy and Hallie. "He was really brave—and shiny."

Hallie and Stuffy are excited when Doc comes back from Donny's room. They want to meet the knight.

Doc sets the toy knight on the floor and brings him to life.
"It is I, Sir Kirby, the **bravest knight** in all of
McStuffins Kingdom," he says with a knightly bow.

Doc and the other toys are surprised when they get a closer look at Sir Kirby. He's rather **dirty**.

"We thought you were going to be a lot . . . shinier," Hallie gently tells the knight.

"Alas, my armor has seen shinier days," Sir Kirby says. "I am still a brave knight." He races to rescue Princess Lambie from the castle—but ends up falling over and getting stuck to the rug.

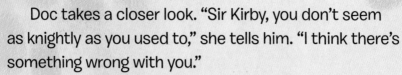

Doc takes a closer look. "Sir Kirby, you don't seem as knightly as you used to," she tells him. "I think there's something wrong with you."

Sir Kirby agrees. "You may be right, Lady McStuffins. My arms and legs aren't working quite the way they should."

Sir Kirby steps forward . . .
and gets stuck to Doc! "I fear
I cannot be the knight I once
was," he says sadly.

"You know how you're really great at saving princesses?" Doc asks the knight as she walks over to her doctor's bag. "Well, I'm really great at saving toys. I promise I'm going to figure out what's wrong with you and make you better. The Doc is in!"

First, Doc checks Sir Kirby's heartbeat. His heart sounds great, but the stethoscope gets stuck.

Next, Sir Kirby stands against a wall so Doc can measure his height.

"Now please come over to my doctor's bag so I can check one more thing," Doc tells Sir Kirby.

The toy knight tries to step away from the wall, but he's stuck. Again. "Perhaps I can have a little help here?" he asks. Stuffy tugs and pulls. Finally, Sir Kirby flies off the wall . . . and gets stuck to the rug again.

Doc lifts Sir Kirby up. "You seem to be sticking to everything," she tells him. "I need to figure out why." She examines the knight from head to toe with her magnifying glass. "It looks like you're covered in grape jelly and pizza cheese," Doc declares.

"Yum!" says Stuffy.

"When was the last time you took a bath?" Doc asks Sir Kirby.

"Uh . . . well, let me see. . . . To tell you the truth, I don't think I've ever taken a bath," the knight admits.

"I have a diagnosis!" Doc announces. "You have Filthy-Icky-Sticky Disease. You're covered with sticky food, and your arms and legs aren't moving well. That means that you, Sir Kirby, are not clean."

Sir Kirby hangs his head in shame. "An unclean knight will never do. I beg you to forgive me, but I shall hand in my armor and go."

"You don't have to stop being a knight," Doc tells him. "We can treat Filthy-Icky-Sticky Disease by giving you a bath and getting you squeaky-clean."

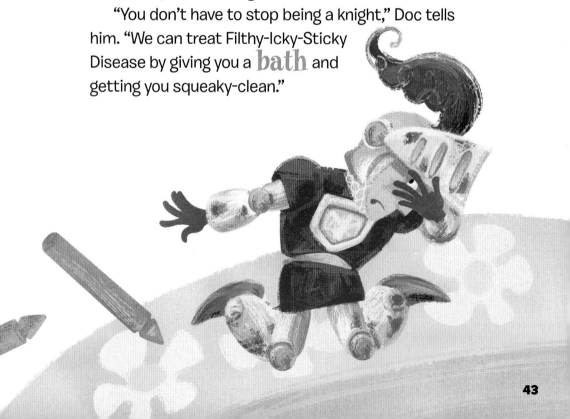

Doc and Sir Kirby head to the bathroom, where Doc's mother is waiting to give them a bath. They wash up with soap and rinse with clean water.

Sir Kirby likes the **bubbles.**

45

After drying off, Doc and Sir Kirby go back to the bedroom. Stuffy, Lambie, and Hallie **cheer** for the improved and very clean Sir Kirby.

"Thanks to you, Lady McStuffins, I feel like myself again," the knight tells Doc.

"You're welcome," says Doc. "Your Filthy-Icky-Sticky Disease is cured!"

Doc decides it is time to play princess once again.

Lambie heads back to the top of the castle. "Oh, no! There are scary dragons everywhere!" she cries.

"Fear not—I shall protect you!" says Sir Kirby as he marches toward Stuffy.

The toy dragon roars his fiercest roar, but then notices his reflection in the knight's shiny armor and is scared.

"Ahh! A dragon!" Stuffy runs away.

"Oh, Sir Kirby, you are so brave!" exclaims Lambie.

"All in a day's work for the **cleanest** knight in all of McStuffins Kingdom!" Sir Kirby declares.

Thanks to Doc McStuffins and a bubbly bath, Sir Kirby has finally saved the princess.

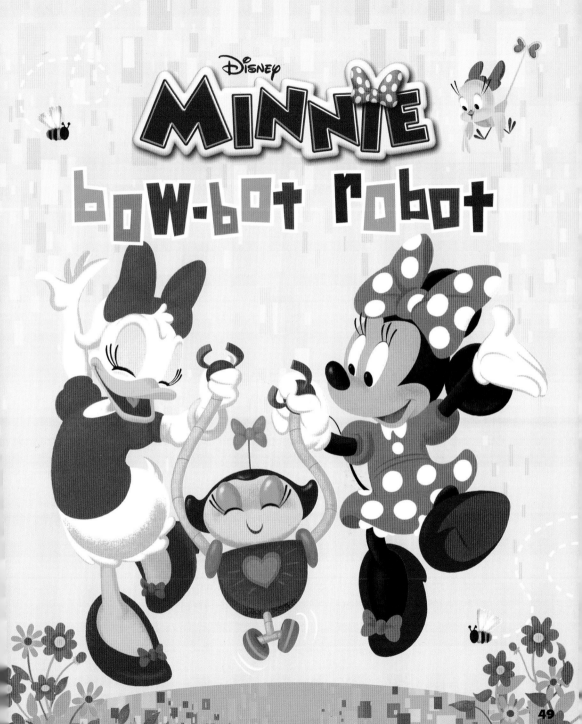

M innie is busy making Bumble Bee Bows in her bow-tique. She has a very big order to complete!

"Mrs. Beary called to say she needs two dozen more for the honey festival," Minnie tells Cuckoo-Loca.

"Two dozen more?" exclaims the cuckoo bird.

"Don't worry," Minnie tells her feathered friend.
"I'll get them done on time . . . somehow."

Just then, Daisy arrives at the shop. "Are you two busy bees ready to take the day off?" she asks Minnie and Cuckoo-Loca.

"That would be nice," Minnie says, "but we've got lots of bows to make."

"Not anymore, you don't!" declares Daisy as she puts a big box on the craft table.

"Ta-daaa!" cries Daisy as she opens the box. She pulls out an adorable little robot with a shiny bow on her head. "I'd like you to meet Bow-Bot, our new bow-making robot!"

"She looks simply wonderful!" Minnie exclaims, admiring her sleek new helper.

"She's super *bow*-tastic!" says Cuckoo-Loca.

"Watch this!" Daisy announces.

She presses a button on the remote
control and Bow-Bot lights up and talks!
"Greetings, M-M-M-Minnie!" says Bow-Bot.
"May I help you with your B-B-B-Bumble Bee Bows?"
"Why, yes!" Minnie says. "Thank you, Bow-Bot!"

Bow-Bot gathers a bunch of ribbon. In no time at all, she makes a display of perfect bows. "Making bows is what I know!" Bow-Bot says proudly.

"Wow! She's fast!" says Cuckoo-Loca.

"Want to see Bow-Bot go even faster?" Daisy asks her friends. She raises the lever on the remote control and pushes another button. Bow-Bot's bow flashes red. Now she's set to go really, really fast!

"Super speed is what we need!" says Bow-Bot.
Bow-Bot works so quickly, she soon runs out of ribbon.

But Bow-Bot doesn't stop.
She makes a bow out of Minnie's chair!

She makes a bow out of the curtains!

She even makes a bow out of the ladder!

"M-m-m-making bows is what I know!" says Bow-Bot, zipping around the store faster and faster.

"Daisy!" exclaims Minnie. "If we don't turn her off, the Bow-tique will be destroyed!"

Daisy tries to stop Bow-Bot, but the remote control's buttons pop out with a loud **SPROING!**

Minnie and Daisy need a plan before things get even worse.

Minnie notices a button on Bow-Bot's back. It's the **OFF** button! But Bow-Bot doesn't stand still long enough for Minnie or Daisy to push it.

"Leave it to me!" Cuckoo-Loca says. She flies over to the button and . . .

. . . Bow-Bot wraps the bird in orange ribbon and speeds away!

"If only Bow-Bot's button weren't so hard to reach!"
Daisy cries.

Minnie sees her *bow*-tastic bow grabber on the table.
She has an idea! "Daisy, you keep Bow-Bot busy," she says.
"I'll take care of the rest."

Daisy grabs some ribbon and holds it up for Bow-Bot to see. "Hey, Bow-Bot!" Daisy calls. "Looking for this?"

Bow-Bot sees the ribbon and zips right over to Daisy.
"Pretty, shiny ribbon! Yes, please!" she says.

While Bow-Bot stands still to look at the ribbon, Minnie uses her bow-grabber to push Bow-Bot's power button. It works! Bow-Bot finally rolls to a stop.

"Poor Bow-Bot," says Cuckoo-Loca sadly.
"It wasn't her fault."
    Minnie looks at the broken remote. Maybe
there's something she can do to fix Bow-Bot.

Minnie uses a screwdriver to make some repairs to the remote and to Bow-Bot. Before she is done, she ties a beautiful ribbon around the remote.

Minnie gives Daisy the new, improved remote control. "Now give it a try, Daisy!" Minnie says.

Daisy presses a button on the remote and Bow-Bot lights up again. "Making bows is what I know!" Bow-Bot says. She is working again—at her regular speed!

"Well, Minnie!" cries Daisy. "Looks like we're back on track."

"Thanks to Bow-Bot!" giggles Minnie. "You know, there really is no business like **b-b-b-bow** business!"

Boomer Gets
His Bounce Back

Doc and her friend Emmie are playing soccer. Doc pretends to be a sports announcer. "World-famous soccer star Emmie lines up for the kick. She shoots. . . . She scores!"

Emmie jumps up and down, celebrating her goal. She gives the ball to Doc. "Hmm, the ball felt a little squishy when I kicked it," she tells Doc.

"Really? Let me try," says Doc.

Doc kicks the ball. It flies through the air, but it lands with a weak little bounce and **s-l-o-w-l-y** rolls into the net.

"Way to go, Doc!" shouts Emmie. "You scored a goal!"

But Doc doesn't celebrate. She checks the ball. It is squishier than it should be. "You're right, Emmie," Doc tells her friend. "Something *is* wrong with the ball."

"But we can't stop playing now," says Emmie. "The next kick is for the world championship!"

Doc pretends to be an announcer again.

"Emmie, the best player in the universe, steps up to the ball. Nothing can stop her!"

Emmie gives the ball a **BIG** kick. But it barely moves. It wobbles and rolls and then stops. It doesn't even reach the net!

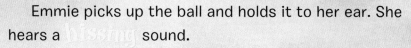

Emmie picks up the ball and holds it to her ear. She hears a *hissing* sound.

"I think it has a leak," Emmie says. "You're the best toy fixer there is, Doc. Can you fix it?"

"I'm pretty sure I can," Doc tells Emmie. "And when I get back, we can finish our championship soccer match."

hissss

Doc goes to her clinic and sets the ball down on the
check-up table. She puts on her magic stethoscope.
It glows—and all the toys in the room come to life!

"Hi, guys! I'm Boomer," the ball announces.
"I know you! You're the best bouncing ball I've
ever seen!" says Stuffy.

"I love to bounce," Boomer tells all the toys, "but I'm not feeling so bouncy today."

Boomer leaps off the table and lands on the ground with a THUD.

"I should bounce back into the air with a BOING," Boomer says with a sigh. "Why can't I bounce, Doc?"

"I'd like to give you a check-up to see what's going on," Doc tells the ball.

Boomer is nervous. "Ooh. A check-up? Uh . . . now that I think about it, I don't need to bounce."

"You're not scared, are you?" Lambie asks gently.

"No way! I don't get scared. I'm totally not scared," Boomer insists.

"So you'll let me give you a check-up?" Doc asks.

"I guess so." Boomer sighs.

Doc begins the check-up by listening to Boomer's heart
with her stethoscope. "Your heart sounds okay," she reports.

Next, she looks at Boomer's throat with her otoscope.
"Your throat looks fine, too."

When Doc asks Hallie for her next tool, Boomer pulls away and cries, "No, you don't need that!"

"Don't worry. I just need the cuff to check your pressure," Doc tells Boomer as Hallie hands it to her.

"Oh, that. Yeah, go for it," says Boomer, relaxing a bit.

"Hmm . . . Boomer, your pressure is way, way, way down." Doc thinks for a moment and then announces, "Hallie, I have a diagnosis!"

Hallie grabs the *Big Book of Boo-Boos* from the shelf and brings it to Doc.

"Boomer, you have a severe case of Deflate-ulosis!" Doc tells her patient.

Boomer gulps.

"What is that?" asks Lambie.

"Everyone has things that belong on their insides," Doc explains. "Stuffy, Lambie, and Chilly have stuffing. But, Boomer, you're a bouncy ball. You need to be full of air to bounce right."

Doc reaches into her doctor bag. "The first thing I need to do to cure Deflate-ulosis is patch your leak."

Boomer holds still as Doc covers the hole with a patch. "Thanks, Doc! Now I'm ready to go back and play!" Boomer says.

"Not yet," says Doc. "I still have to put more air back inside you."

"Naw, that's all right. I'm good," Boomer claims as he tries to roll away.

Doc thinks she knows why Boomer is scared. "Have you been filled with air before?" she asks the ball.

Boomer nods.

"And you know I'm going to use an air pump?" Doc asks as she pulls a pump from her doctor bag.

"And it has a needle," Boomer says with a sigh. "I'm scared of needles!"

Doc explains that she has to use the needle—it's the only way to fill Boomer back up. Chilly jumps in front of Doc. "Oh, no! I think I need more air inside me, too!" he claims.

"Chilly, you're not a ball," Doc reminds him. Then she turns back to Boomer. But he's gone!

Doc and the toys look all over for Boomer. Finally, Lambie finds the ball hiding inside the dollhouse. "I think you need a cuddle," she tells him as she gives him a big hug.

Doc kneels next to Boomer. "Want to know a secret? When I need to get a shot with a needle from *my* doctor, I'm always scared," she admits. "But my mom comes and gives me a big hug, and that helps me to be brave."

"I like hugs," says Boomer.

"We could *all* give you a hug!" suggests Lambie.

"That should help you feel brave," Doc says.

Hallie, Lambie, Chilly, and Stuffy give Boomer a big hug. Boomer says he feels better already. "Let's do this!"

Doc inserts the needle and starts pumping. "You're being really, really brave!" she tells Boomer.

Boomer starts to get **bigger** as he is filled with more air. "I can feel myself getting bouncier and bouncier!" he shouts.

"Now you should be back to your bold, bouncy self!" Doc declares.

"Thanks for the cuddles," Boomer tells the toys, "but can you un-hug me now? This ball can't wait to bounce!"

Boomer bounces high into the air. He bounces off the dollhouse. He bounces right over Doc and the toys!

"Thank you, Doc!" Boomer yells as he continues bouncing. "I don't know if you knew this, but I *love* bouncing!"

"Aren't you glad you were brave?" asks Stuffy.

"I sure am," admits Boomer. "A few seconds of being brave and now I'm back to bouncing way, way, way high! This is great!"

Doc giggles. "It's great to have you back in bouncing shape," she tells the happy ball. "Now let's go meet up with Emmie so we can finish our world championship soccer match!"

BUNNY MAGIC!

It's a lovely day in Enchancia. Princess Sofia and her pet bunny, Clover, are playing hide-and-seek in the royal vegetable garden. Suddenly, Sofia notices a pile of radishes that seems to be moving. "Found you!" Sofia cries. "That was good—until you started to eat your hiding place," she adds with a giggle.

"Okay, Princess," says Clover. "Now it's your turn to hide."

"I wish I could, but I don't have time," Sofia replies as she heads off to archery class.

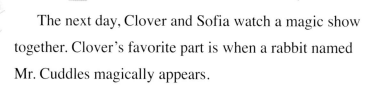

The next day, Clover and Sofia watch a magic show together. Clover's favorite part is when a rabbit named Mr. Cuddles magically appears.

After the show, Clover hops in front of the princess and announces, "Now I, the Amazing Clover, am about to take you on an afternoon of adventure!"

Just then, Minimus the flying pony arrives to take Sofia to Flying Derby practice.

"Sorry, Clover," says the princess as she puts on her riding outfit. "We'll do something later, okay?"

Robin and Mia swoop down to cheer Clover up as he sadly watches Sofia and Minimus fly away.

Clover perks up a bit when he notices Mr. Cuddles hop by. "Hey, great show!" he calls to the magician's rabbit.

"Thanks, but I'm quitting," replies Mr. Cuddles. "I want to be a serious actor, not a magician's prop. You want the job? It's yours."

Clover thinks being a magic rabbit sounds like fun. "And anyway, Sofia will be too busy to even notice I'm gone," he tells Robin and Mia. The little birds try to convince Clover to stay, but his mind is made up. He jumps on the magician's wagon. "Farewell!" he says as it rolls out the kingdom gates.

The next morning, Sofia is surprised to find Clover's bed empty.

"He joined the magic show," Robin tells the princess. "He said you didn't need him around anymore."

Sofia is stunned. "That's not true!" she exclaims. "I've got to find Clover and ask him to come home!" She puts on her riding clothes and rushes to the stable.

Sofia asks Minimus to help her find Clover. Crackle
wants to go, too. "You never know when a dragon will come
in handy!" Crackle says.

The friends zoom through the sky, searching the roads for
a red covered wagon.

Meanwhile, Clover is backstage after finishing his first magic show. He admits to the magician's dove that he loves the applause but he really misses Sofia.

"Hey, I left some friends behind, too," the dove tells Clover. "But this is better. We're big stars now!"

Clover isn't sure he agrees.

A little later, Sophia, Minimus, and Crackle land near a red covered wagon. "Oh, it's not the magician," Sofia says sadly when she spots a woman with a crystal ball.

"I am better than a magician!" announces the woman. "I am Madame Ubetcha, the greatest fortune-teller!"

Sofia tells Madame Ubetcha that they are looking for her pet rabbit. The fortune-teller peers into her crystal ball and says, "Crystal ball, don't be funny. Help me find this girl's bunny!" Suddenly, an image of Clover appears inside the glowing ball. Next to him is a fancy tower.

"I've seen that tower before!" declares Sofia. "It's in Somerset Village."

"Let's go! Let's go!" cries Crackle.

After thanking the fortune-teller, the friends race off.

Meanwhile, Clover has been telling the dove story after story about his friend Sofia.

"Hey, kid," the dove interrupts, "if you two had so much fun together, why did you leave?"

"She got busy and didn't have time for me," Clover admits.

"Most people get busy," replies the dove. "That doesn't mean they love you any less."

"I'm going home," Clover says, and he hops toward the exit door.

But the magician stops him. "I'm not about to have another bunny run out on me," he says, stuffing Clover into his hat. "Five minutes till showtime!"

"Clover!"

After the magician goes onstage, Clover hears a friendly voice call his name.

"I've been looking for you everywhere!" exclaims Sofia. "I'm sorry I wasn't spending enough time with you. If you come back, I'll make it up to you."

Clover leaps into Sofia's arms for a hug.

Then the magician returns. "What are you doing with my magic bunny?" he demands, snatching Clover from Sofia. "If you want to see him, feel free to buy a ticket to the show."

Clover's eyes fill with tears as he is put back into the hat and carried onstage.

Luckily, Sofia has seen this magic act before—and she comes up with a plan. "All I need to do is volunteer for the last trick and Clover will appear right in my arms!" she tells her friends. "But I need a disguise."

Madame Ubetcha suddenly appears, holding out a yellow cloak. "I *knew* you would need this," the fortune-teller says.

Sofia pulls the hood of the cloak over her head. She finds a seat in the audience just as the magician asks for a volunteer for his grand finale.

The princess raises her hand and calls out, "Me! Me!" in a deep voice. The magician calls her to the stage. Even Clover doesn't recognize her.

"Let the amazement begin!" shouts the magician. He puts Clover in a box and closes the curtain. When the curtain is opened again, Clover is gone!

"Now, young lady," the magician says to Sofia, "it is your turn to step inside."

Sofia steps in. After the curtain is closed, a hidden panel in the box rotates, and Sofia and Clover are together! She takes off her hood and whispers, "I'm here to rescue you!"

The magician pulls back the curtain. He peeks through the back of the box and sees Sofia and Clover running away. "Come back with my magic bunny!" he yells.

Sofia and Clover jump on Minimus's back. But the magician grabs hold of Clover before the pony can take off. Robin and Mia block his path. As the magician turns, Crackle swoops down and lets out a burst of flames. The magician yelps and drops Clover.

Crackle catches the bunny, and his friends cheer. "I told you it
would be handy to have a dragon around," Crackle says proudly.

Clover thanks everyone for saving him.

"Next time you have a problem, promise you'll come talk to me before you go off and join a magic show," Sofia tells her furry friend.

"You got it!" replies Clover. Then he cuddles up to Sofia as Minimus flies them back home.

A Skipping Day

It's a nice day on Shipwreck Beach. Jake and his crew are playing with a jump rope.

"Yay hey! This jump rope is fun!" Izzy says.

"It's awesome!" Jake agrees.

Skully flutters this way and that way, happily
flying under the rope when he gets a chance.

Jake, Izzy, and Skully don't know it, but Captain Hook is spying on them with his spyglass.

"Those puny pirates are having fun with that jumpy thing," says Hook. "I want to have fun, too!"

"I must have that jumpy thing," Captain Hook tells his first mate, Mr. Smee. "Get me that treasure!" Mr. Smee salutes Hook and says, "Yes, Cap'n!"

Meanwhile, back on the beach, the pirate crew is ready for a healthy snack.

"It's smoothie time, mateys!" announces Cubby.

"Thanks, Cubby," says Izzy. "All that jumping has made me thirsty."

"Those look great, Cubby!" says Jake.
 Jake puts the jump rope on the sand. After he
and his friends drink their smoothies, they will
jump some more.

Jake, Izzy, and Skully head over to Cubby.
"Crackers! I love smoothies!" says Skully.

As the pirates enjoy their drinks, Captain Hook and Smee sneak onto the beach. "The jumpy thing is mine, Smee!" Hook declares.

Skully spots the scoundrels. "It's Captain Hook!" he cries.

Jake turns just in time to see Hook and Smee running away.

"Hey! He stole our jump rope!" Izzy says as Captain Hook and Smee head into Tiki Tree Forest.

"Yo ho! Let's get our treasure back!" declares Jake.

The pirate crew rushes to catch up with Hook and Smee. Unfortunately, a river stops them in their tracks.

"Aw, coconuts! How did Hook and Smee get to the other side of this river?" Cubby asks.

Izzy thinks for a moment. Then she comes up with a solution.
"We'll jump on the stones to cross the river," she says.
Jake thinks it's a great idea. "Yo ho! Way to go!"

"Let's do it on the count of three," says Izzy. "One, two, three!"

Jake, Izzy, and Cubby jump on the rocks and cross the river. Skully cheers them on. "Crackers! You're doing it!" calls the parrot.

Everyone is having fun. "I love jumping!" exclaims Cubby.

When they reach the other side of the river, Jake and his crew quickly catch up to Captain Hook and Mr. Smee.

"Please give us back our jump rope, Captain Hook!" cries Jake.

"Never!" Captain Hook says. "It's my turn to have fun!"

Hook is all set to finally play with the jump rope. Izzy notices that the rope is tangled around his feet. "Watch out, Hook!" Izzy warns.

But Captain Hook doesn't listen.
He falls to the ground, all tied up.
"Smee!" Hook cries. "Save meee!"

Izzy and Jake rush over to help. In no time, the
friends free Captain Hook from the jump rope.

"Barnacles! That jumpy thing is broken," Captain Hook declares. "I don't want it anymore."

"It's not broken," Jake says, smiling.

"We'll teach you how to use it," Izzy adds.

The jolly buccaneers show Captain Hook and Smee what to do. Before long, they're all jumping—and having fun!

"I'm jumping, Smee! I'm jumping!" shouts Hook happily.

"Well done, Cap'n," says Smee.

The Perfect Tea Party

It's an exciting day at Royal Prep—the fairies are choosing which student will host the annual school tea party.

Sofia's new stepsister, Amber, explains that Royal Prep tea parties are really big events. "They have merry-go-rounds, ponies, and even hot-air balloons!"

Sofia has never been to a royal tea party. She just recently became a princess when her mother married King Roland.

In class, Sofia's teacher, Flora, holds out a teapot. "Only students who haven't had a chance to host a party should submit their names," says the fairy.

Sofia excitedly drops a slip of paper with her name on it into the teapot.

Flora uses her wand to stir the pot. Soon one paper
magically floats out.

"The host of the next Royal Prep tea party will be . . .
Princess Sofia!" she announces.

Sofia is thrilled.

"You can throw any kind of party you like," Flora tells her.
"This is your chance to show us who you are."

Sofia

On the ride home from school, Sofia talks about the tea party with Amber and her stepbrother, James. "There have already been so many big, fancy tea parties," she says. "I'd like to throw a simple tea party like I used to in the village. My friends and I would spread blankets on the ground and borrow teacups from our mothers."

James thinks that sounds cool. Amber doesn't. "No one wants to use borrowed teacups!" she exclaims. "When it comes to royal parties, the bigger the better!"

Sofia starts to think that maybe Amber is right. She spots the swan fountain and tells Baileywick, the castle caretaker, that she would like to have a swan-themed tea party. "We'll have swan-shaped cookies and cakes."

"That sounds lovely," says Baileywick. Amber likes the swan theme but encourages Sofia to think even bigger.

"Hmm. Maybe Cedric, the Royal Sorcerer, can make the tables and chairs float in the air like swans float on water," suggests Sofia. "And the swans can put on a show."

"That's more like it!" says Amber.

Later that day, Sofia is visited by her friends from the village, Jade and Ruby. Even though Sofia is busy planning the Royal Prep tea party, she is happy to take a break to spend time with them.

"Let's have a little snack," Sofia suggests. "I know the perfect spot."

Sofia leads Jade and Ruby along a row of hedges. Then she pushes aside some ivy, uncovering a wooden door. The door opens and the girls step into Sofia's secret garden.

"It's beautiful!" says Ruby.

"Look at all the butterflies!" cries Jade.

The girls spread out a blanket and share a plate of cookies. "This reminds me of the tea parties we had in the village," Ruby says. "Are you throwing a party like this for your princess friends?"

Sofia sighs. "I want to, but they expect a big, fancy tea party."

"That's too bad, because I'm having a great time just doing this," says Ruby.

"Me too," agrees Sofia.

After a few more cookies, Sofia sadly says good-bye and gets back to her party planning.

"Ah, Princess Sofia, you're just in time to choose the plates for your party," Baileywick says as Sofia enters the dining room.

Sofia looks at all the choices. She likes the simple white ones.

Amber shakes her head and holds up a large, shiny golden plate. "You need something like this," she declares. "Remember, bigger is better."

Sofia gives in and agrees to use the large golden plates.

At another table, James is happily munching on a swan-shaped cookie. "These are great!" he declares as crumbs fall from his mouth.

"You should order two hundred of these cookies for the tea party, and make them as big as possible," Amber tells Sofia. "You'll need a huge swan cake, too!"

Sofia thinks it's too much, but she listens to Amber anyway.

Next, Sofia heads to Cedric's workshop.

"I'm hosting a tea party tomorrow, and it would be great if you could make all the tables and chairs rise just a little bit off the ground," Sofia explains to the Royal Sorcerer. "Do you have a spell that can do that?"

Floaticus - hover - a - boo !

Cedric points his wand at a beaker on his worktable. "Floaticus-hover-a-boo!" The beaker twinkles magically and rises into the air.

"That's terrific!" cries Sofia. "See you at the party tomorrow."

Sofia goes to the swan fountain. Luckily, the magical amulet King Roland gave her, the Amulet of Avalar, gives her the power to talk to animals!

"I'm hosting a tea party, and I was hoping you could perform a water ballet," she tells the swans.

"It would be our pleasure," replies Portia.

"Great! See you tomorrow!" says Sofia, and rushes off to find the perfect tea party dress.

As the royal dressmaker hems her gown, Sofia tells her mother about the tea party. "It is going to be so big and fancy. Amber says everyone is going to love it." She sighs. "But part of me wishes I could just have a sweet tea party like the ones I used to have with Ruby and Jade."

"I'm sure everyone will be pleased no matter what kind of party you throw," says Queen Miranda.

The day of Sofia's royal tea party has arrived! As the servants rush about, everything goes wrong. The swan-shaped ice sculpture falls off its cart and slides into the baker, who drops his tray of swan cookies. Then the ice slides into the fountain, scaring the swans.

The swans fly into Cedric just as he is casting his floating spell! The tables and chairs rise off the ground—and float away! Sofia can't believe her eyes!

The princess regrets listening to Amber. Her party is ruined, and the guests are on their way. Sofia starts to cry. Then she spots a butterfly and knows exactly what to do.

When the students and fairies arrive, Baileywick moves aside some ivy, pushes open the wooden door, and welcomes them into Sofia's secret garden. Blankets on the grass have been set with teapots and cups. Butterflies flutter over the flowers. And all the princesses love it—including Amber!

"Nice job, Sofia! I guess bigger isn't always better," Amber admits.

"Princess Sofia, what a charming party!" Flora tells the hostess. "Some peppermint tea, a pretty garden, and a beautiful view. Who could ask for more?"

All the guests raise their teacups and cheer, "To Princess Sofia!"

Sofia is pleased to learn that even princesses can enjoy simple things. She giggles and raises her own teacup. "Hooray for me!"

Snowman Surprise

It's a beautiful winter afternoon, and Doc McStuffins is playing in the snow with her toys.

"I just **love** when it snows!" Doc exclaims.

"Me too!" says Stuffy the stuffed dragon. "I love everything about snow. . . ." Just then, a clump of snow falls from a branch and lands on Stuffy's head.

"Except that."

Chilly, Doc's stuffed snowman, is excited to spend time with a real snowman. "Come on, you can tell me . . . you get cold sometimes, right? I know I d-d-do!" Chilly says with a shiver.

Doc giggles and reminds Chilly that unlike the real snowman, *he* has to bundle up in the cold.

Soon, Doc's dad calls for her to go inside. Doc scoops up Chilly, Lambie, Hallie, and Stuffy and walks to the house.

Once inside, Doc gets out of her **wet** clothes. Her boots, mittens, and scarf are easy to take off, but she needs a little help getting out of her jacket.

Doc runs upstairs to do her homework.
Her dad takes her wet clothes to the laundry room.
Neither of them notices that Chilly is missing.

After dinner, Doc's brother, Donny, shows off the diorama he made for school.

"It's a winter scene," explains Donny. "What do you think?"

Doc takes a look. "You know what it could use? A **snowman**! Do you want to borrow Chilly?"

"That would be cool!" says Donny.

Doc goes to her bedroom to get Chilly, but she doesn't see him. She holds her stethoscope until it glows, making her toys magically come to life.

"Have you seen Chilly?" Doc asks Stuffy, Hallie, and Lambie. "I know I brought him in the house."

Everyone looks around. No Chilly.

"Let's have a **search** party!" suggests Hallie.

Doc and the toys sneak downstairs. "You guys check the living room," Doc says. "I'll go to the laundry room."

Lambie peeks under a couch cushion.

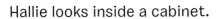

Hallie looks inside a cabinet.

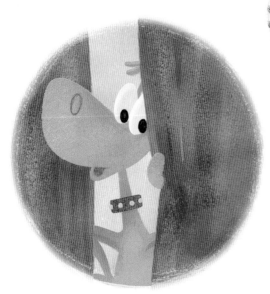

Stuffy peers behind a curtain. No Chilly.

"Chilly? Are you down here?"
Doc calls into the laundry room.
There is no answer. Then, just as
Doc leaves the room to continue
her search, her stethoscope glows.

The **red scarf** starts to move. "Doc? You there?" Chilly asks as he crawls from underneath the scarf. He tumbles off the shelf and lands on the floor with a thud.

"*Oof!* I hope I didn't break any bones," Chilly says to himself. "Oh, wait, I don't have any bones!" Then he notices his arms. They look a bit . . . different!

Chilly rushes into Doc's bedroom. "Maybe it's not so bad," he says, trying to calm down. He nervously peeks at the mirror. "It's worse!" he shouts. "I'm pink all over!"

Chilly hears Doc and the others heading his way. "Oh, no! They'll laugh at me if they see me like this." He runs and hides.

"I'm worried about Chilly. Where could that snowman be?" Hallie asks as she and the others enter Doc's room.

"No need to worry," says Chilly. "Here I am!"

Doc and the toys turn to see Chilly's hat peeking from between some books. "I'm just tidying up back here," he explains.

"Well, I have exciting news," Doc says. "Donny needs a snowman for his project, and he wants you! You're perfect for it!"

Chilly is thrilled that Donny and Doc think he's the perfect snowman. But he's not perfect now—he's pink!

As Doc gets closer to the bookshelf, Chilly jumps into the laundry basket. When he climbs out, he's wearing one of Doc's socks. "*Brrrr,* it's chilly in here," he says.

Doc kneels down. "Chilly, is something wrong?" she asks. "Maybe I should give you a checkup."

Chilly leans closer to Doc and whispers, "There *is* something wrong, but I can't show you in front of everybody."

Doc asks Hallie, Stuffy, and Lambie to give them some privacy. "Okay, we're alone," says Doc. "And you know you can tell your doctor anything. So what's going on?"

Chilly takes off the sock. "This is the worst thing you've ever seen, right?"

Doc reassures Chilly as she examines him. "Everything's okay, except your **color** has changed," Doc says. "I think you have a case of pink-i-tosis. But don't worry. I'm going to fix you."

"I hope so," Chilly says with a sigh. "Donny needs a perfect snowman, and right now I'm not perfect at all."

"Just because you're different doesn't mean you're not perfect!" Doc declares. "Now, can you tell me what happened?"

Chilly starts to cry. "I have no idea! I woke up in the laundry room under your snow clothes and I was pink!"

"That's it!" Doc exclaims. "Dad must have washed you by accident, and the red color from my scarf rubbed off on you! We can get you cleaned up whenever you want!"

Chilly wants to tell everyone that he's okay, so he and Doc go over to the other toys. "No matter what color you are, we love you just the same!" says Hallie as his friends hug him.

Chilly is starting to like his new color. "Do you think Donny would mind a pink snowman in his project?" he asks Doc.

"Let's find out," she says.

Doc shows Chilly to her brother. "A pink snowman? Cool!" says Donny. "No one else is going to have a pink snowman in their project!"

The next day, Donny rushes home with great news.
"Guess what?" he shouts as he hands Chilly to Doc.
"My teacher said using a pink snowman was very creative.
And she gave me a *gold* star!"

   "I'm so proud of you, Donny!" Doc tells her brother.
"And I'm proud of you, too," she whispers to Chilly.

A little later, Doc and her toys go outside to play. Chilly shows the real snowman a photo of himself with the gold star.

"You know, no one should be afraid to be different," Chilly says.

Doc walks over and smiles. "Ready for Dad to clean you now?" she asks.

Chilly nods. "Pink. Red. Green. It's not the color that makes you a snowman—it's the snow. Or, in my case, the stuffing!"

Shop with Minnie

Minnie has invited her friends to see the new items in her store.

"I have bows and bow ties of all shapes, colors, and sizes," Minnie says. "Please come in and shop."

Mickey, Donald, Daisy, Goofy,
Pluto, Clarabelle, and Pete all head
into Minnie's Bow-tique.

Everyone starts to look around. "Gawrsh, Minnie!" says Goofy. "I love your butterfly bows."

Minnie hands Goofy a butterfly net. "I'm having a special today," she tells him. "You can keep all the butterfly bows you catch."

Pete wants to find a birthday present for his aunt. There are so many bows to choose from! He leans over a display to reach for a pretty striped bow and . . .

. . . accidentally knocks all the bows down!
Pete feels bad about making a mess.

Luckily, everything is soon back where it belongs. Pete doesn't want to make any more messes. He decides to see which bows everyone else plans to get. Maybe that will help him find one for his aunt.

Minnie is a great salesperson.
She helps everyone find the bows
that are just right for them.
Pluto has a bone bow—perfect
for a fancy pup!

Donald's bow tie doesn't just look great—it also takes pictures. It's a camera bow!

"Say 'cheese,'" Donald calls out to his friends.

"Attention, everyone!" Mickey loves that his bow tie makes his voice loud enough for everyone to hear. It's a microphone bow!

Clarabelle is crazy about her one-of-a-kind bow. When she sprays it with water, it grows flowers. It's a grow bow!

"Oh, Goofy!" Mickey announces with his microphone bow. "There are more butterfly bows for you to catch."

"This is more fun than a circus!" Goofy exclaims as two butterfly bows flutter on his arms. "Look, everyone—el*bows*!"

"My new bow makes me very happy," Daisy says to Minnie. "I can tell," Minnie replies. "It's a mood bow."

When Daisy is happy,
the mood bow is yellow.

When Daisy is sad,
the bow will turn blue.

When she is angry,
the bow will turn red.

Minnie models her store's fanciest bow.
It's a sparkling, shining disco bow!

All the bows in Minnie's Bow-tique are
great, but Pete still doesn't know which one
to get for his aunt. Then he spots a colorful
bow with a switch attached to it. Pete
gives the switch a tug and the bow starts
spinning. It's a fan bow!

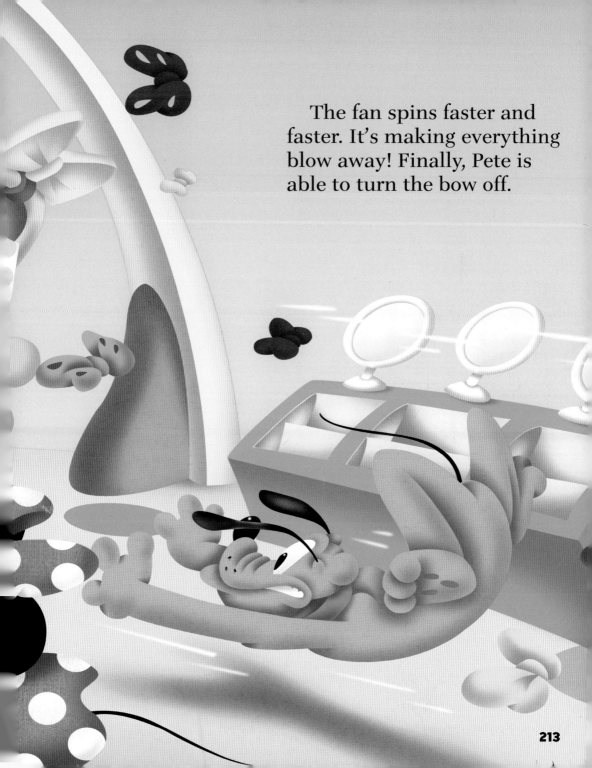

The fan spins faster and faster. It's making everything blow away! Finally, Pete is able to turn the bow off.

Everyone rushes to gather up the bows and return them to the store.

Minnie apologizes to her friends. "I'm sorry about the fan bow," she tells them. "I haven't figured out how to get it to work properly yet."

"I think it's perfect!" cries Pete. "My aunt will love it just the way it is."

He shows Minnie a picture of his aunt.

"She works in a hot kitchen all day long. A fan bow will be the best birthday present ever!"

Minnie is thrilled that all her friends found bows they like at her bow-tique.